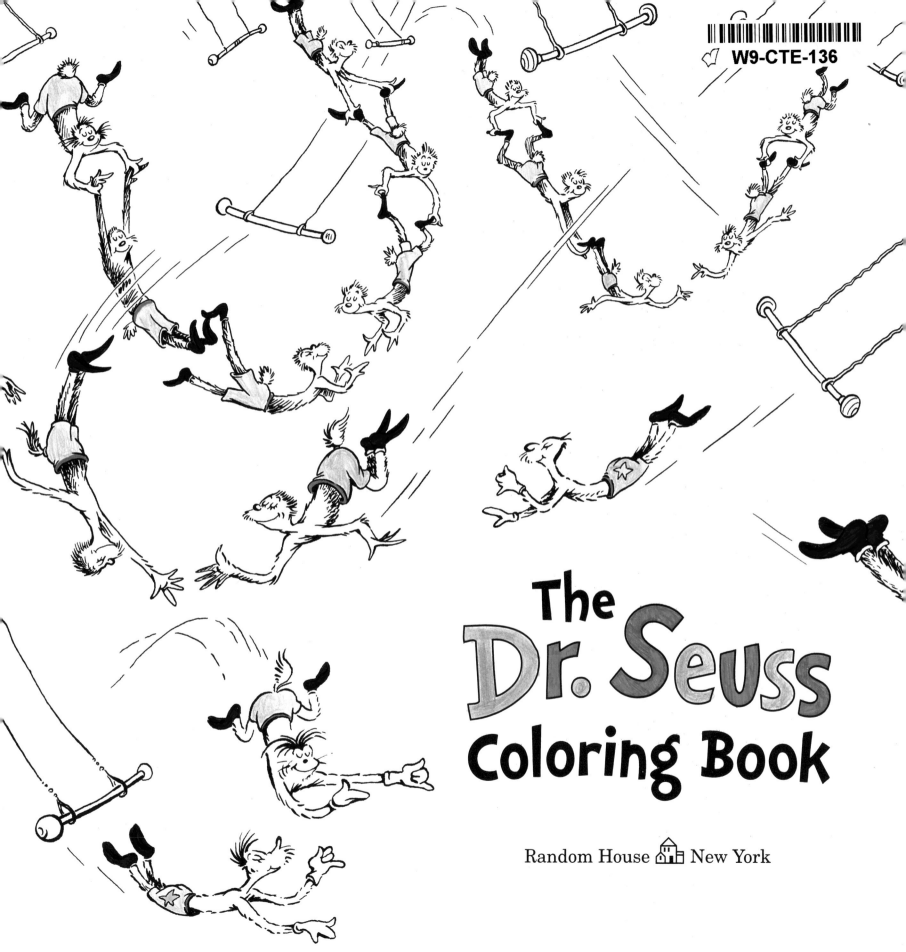

The Dr. Seuss Coloring Book

Random House 🏠 New York

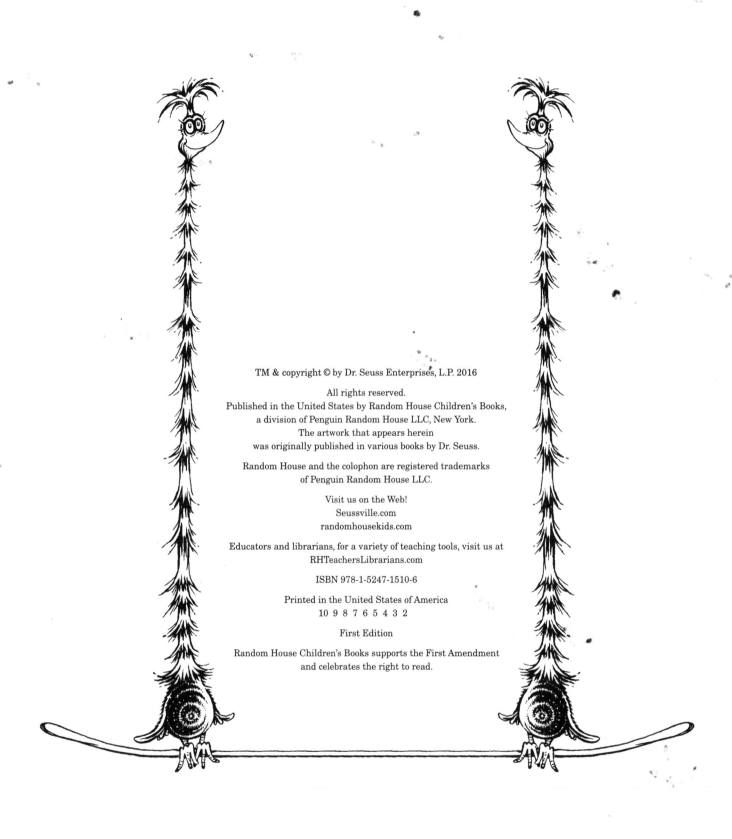

Random House and the colophon are registered trademarks
of Penguin Random House LLC.

Visit us on the Web!
Seussville.com
randomhousekids.com

Educators and librarians, for a variety of teaching tools, visit us at
RHTeachersLibrarians.com

ISBN 978-1-5247-1510-6

Printed in the United States of America
10 9 8 7 6 5 4 3 2

First Edition

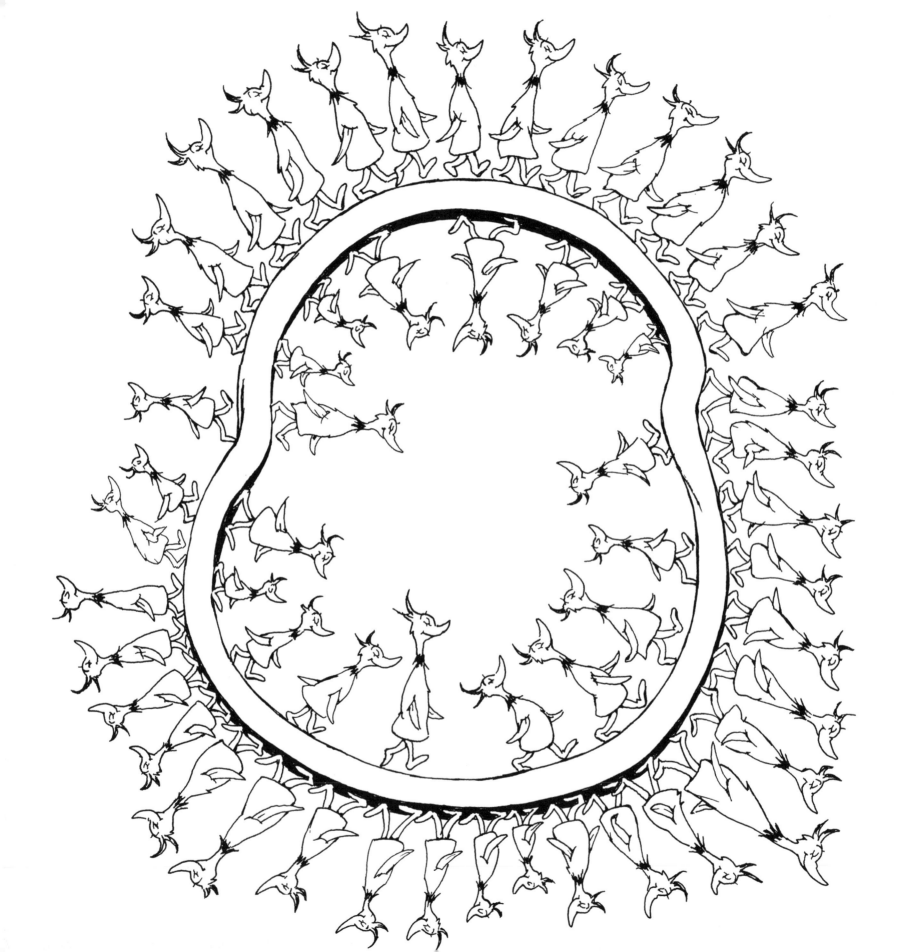

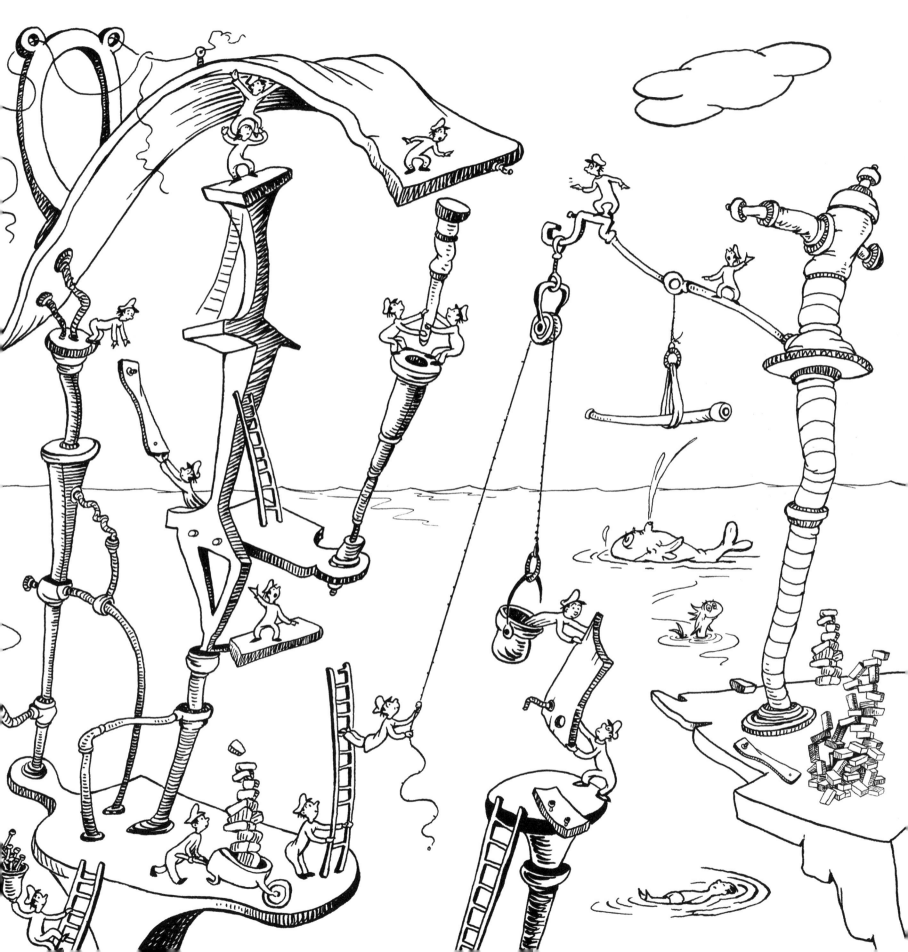

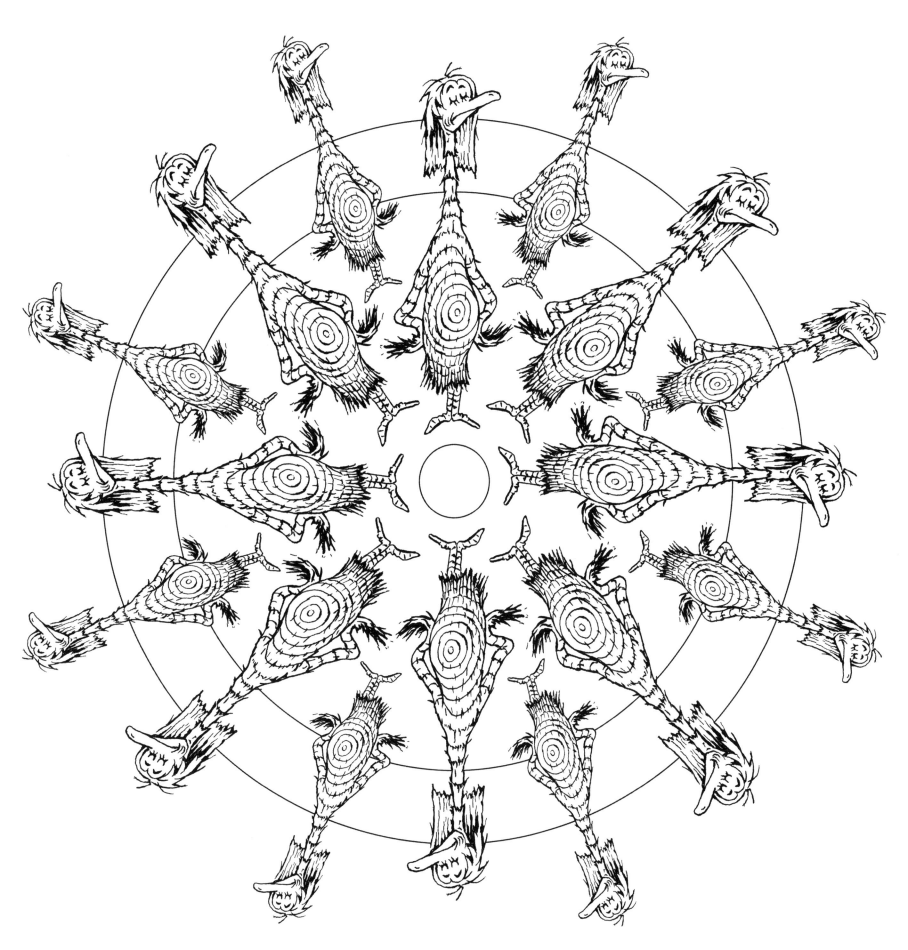

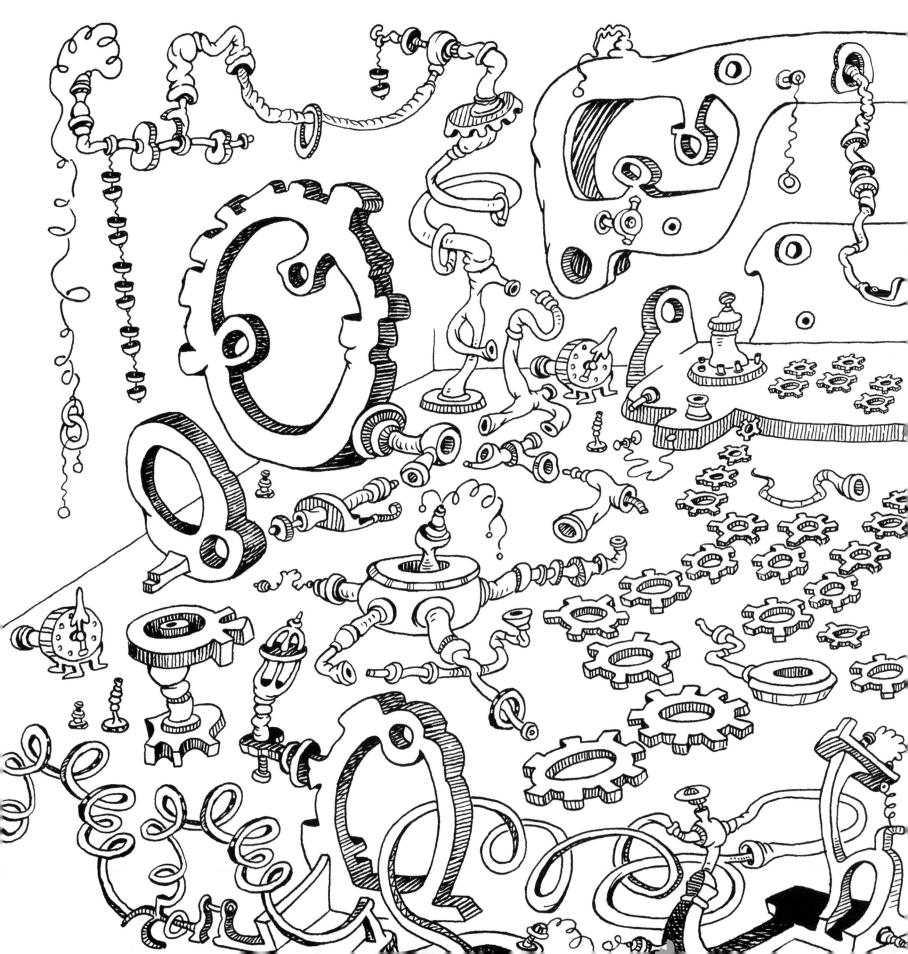

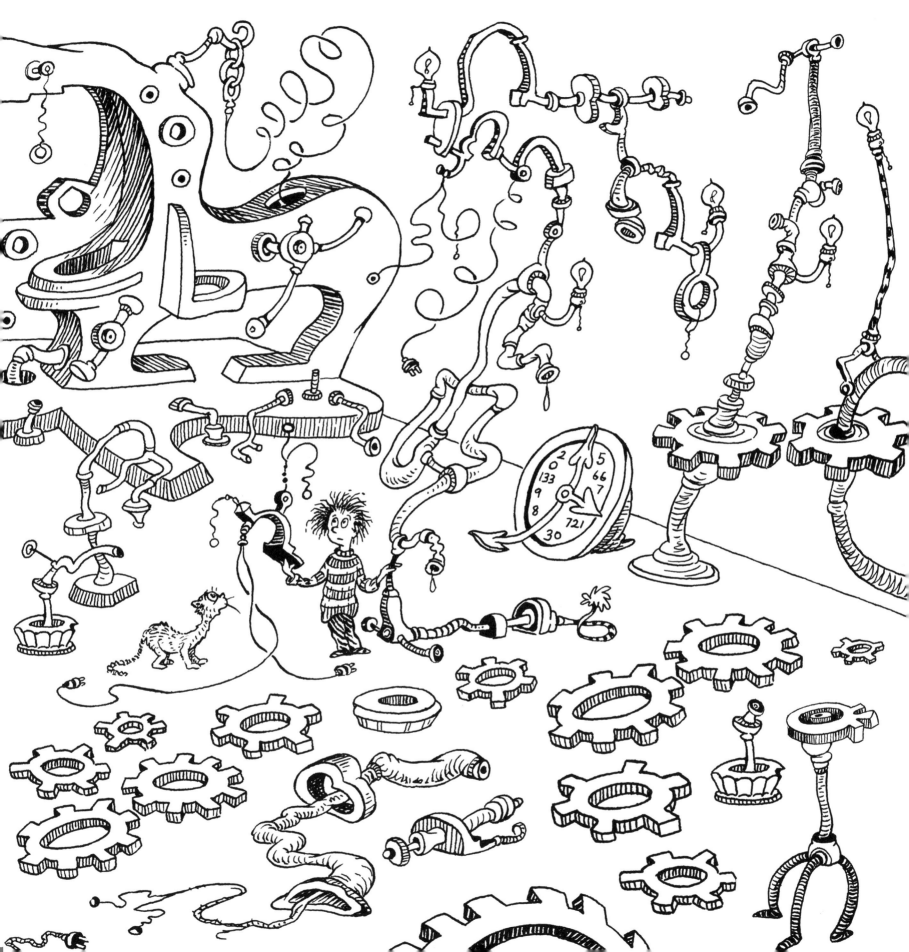

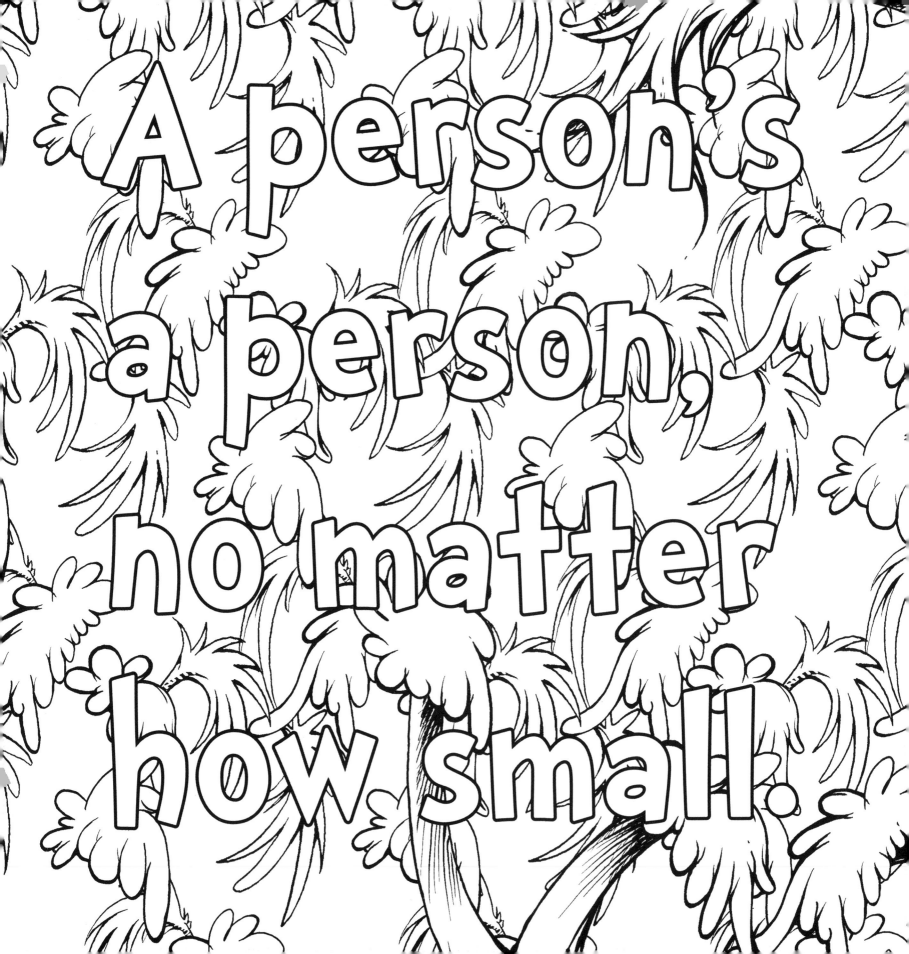

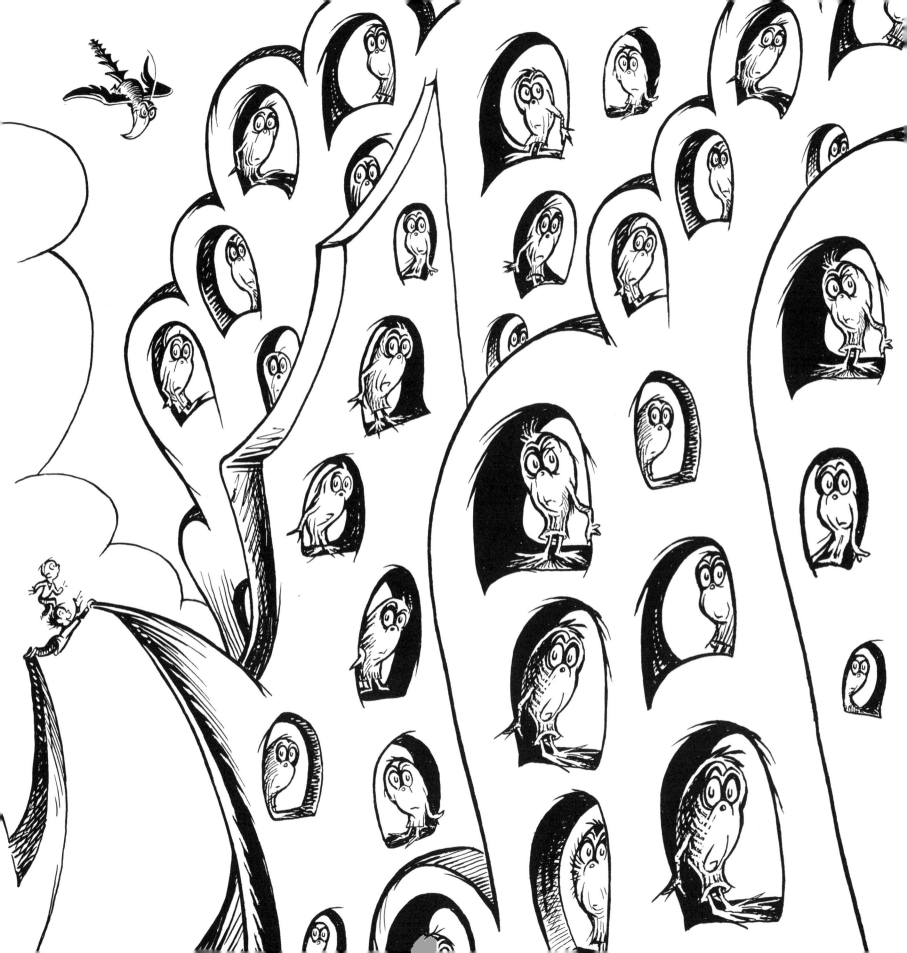

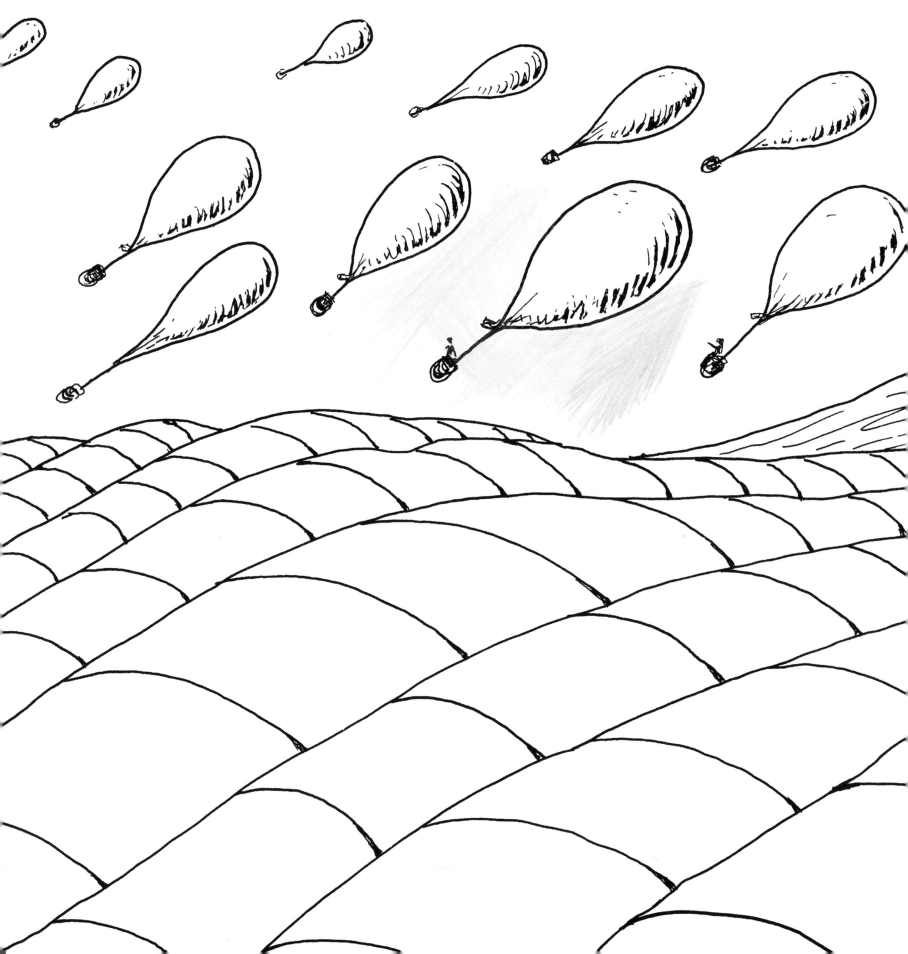

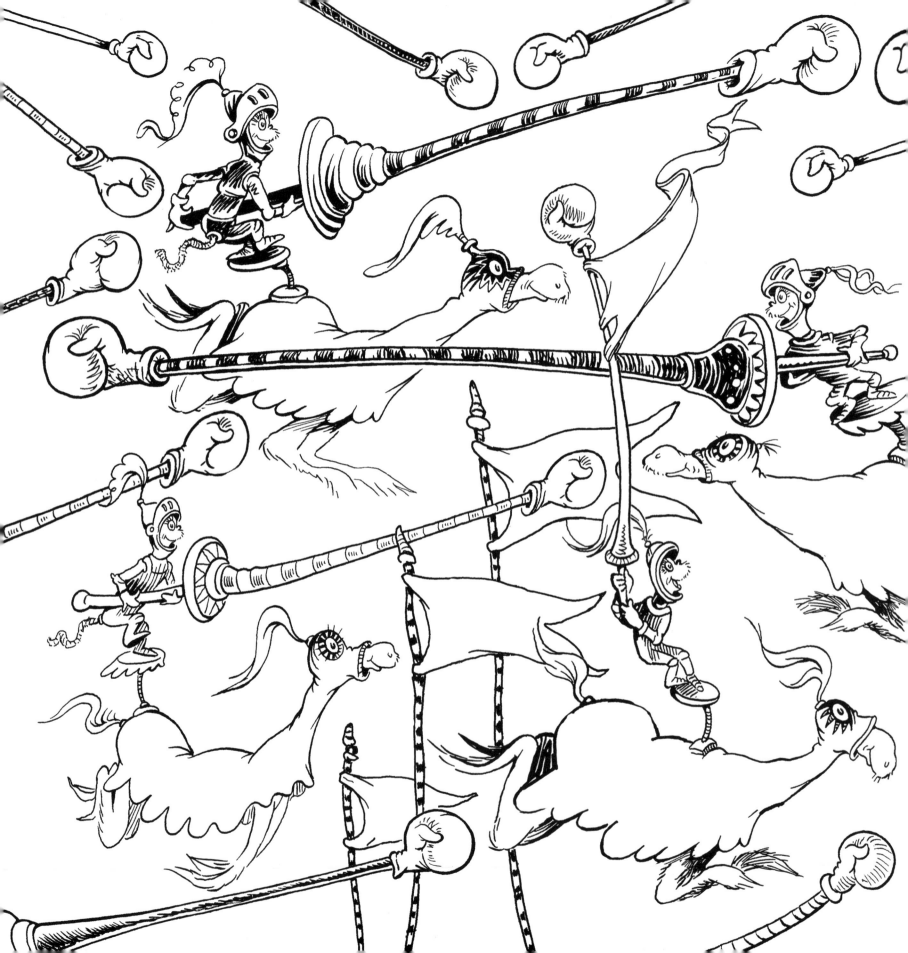

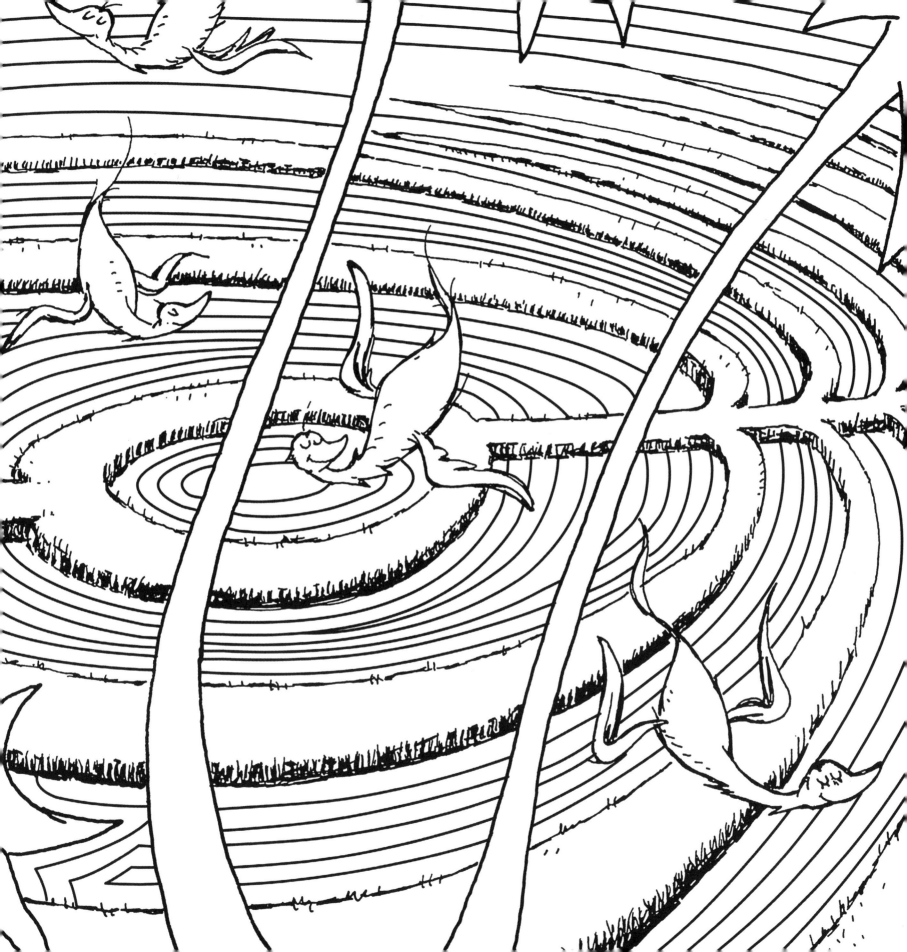

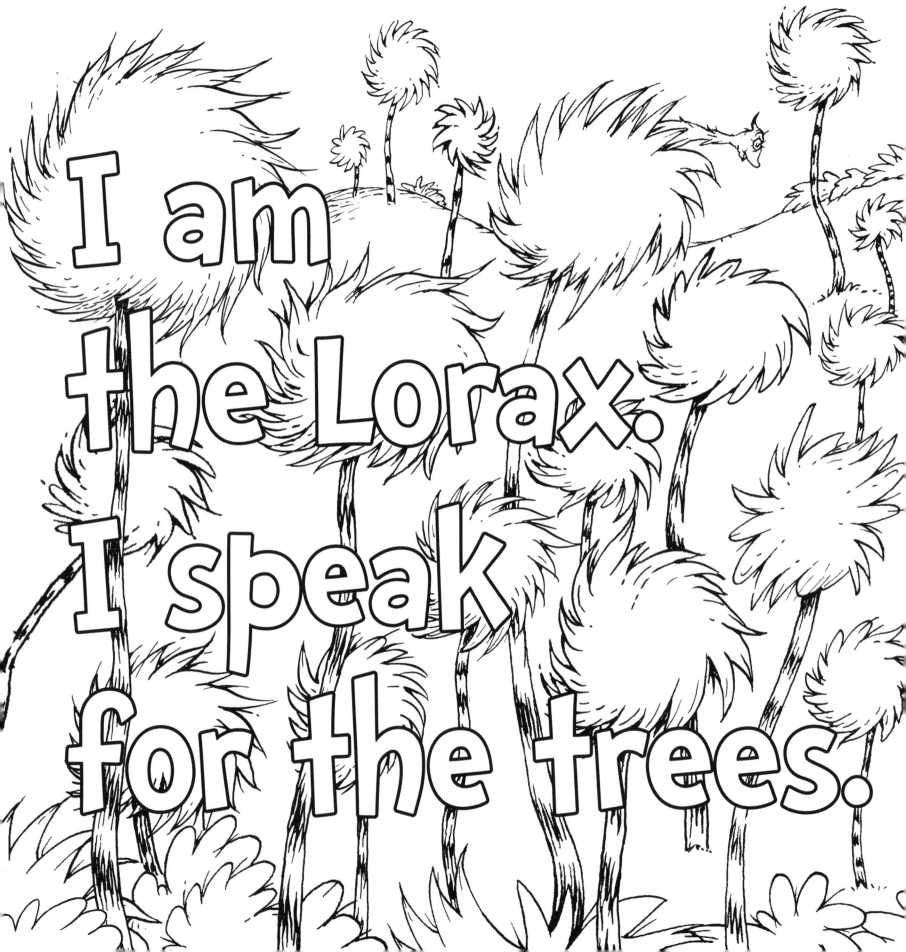

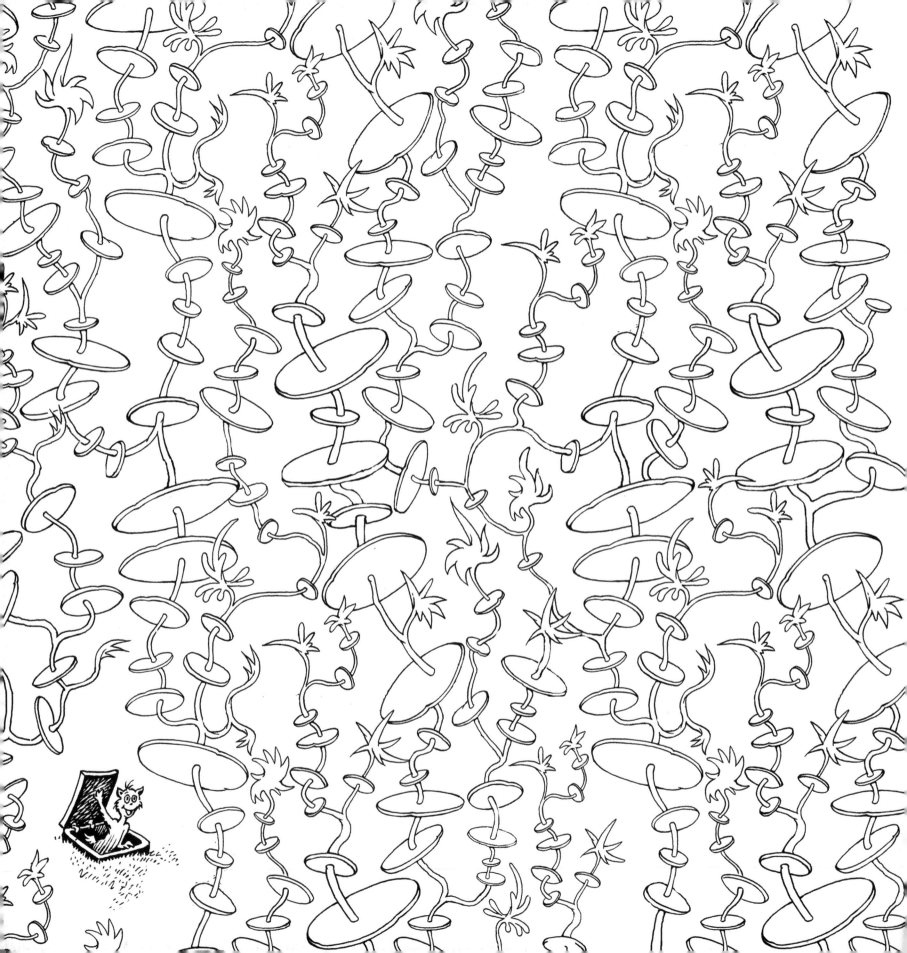

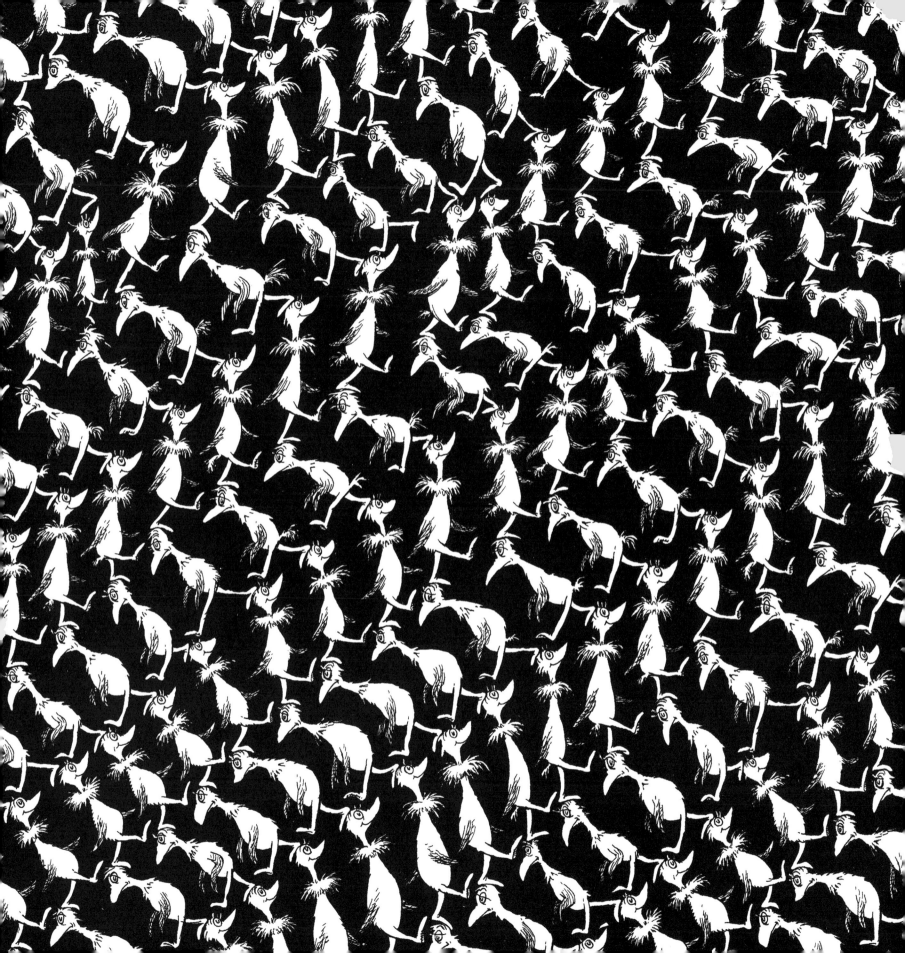

BANG

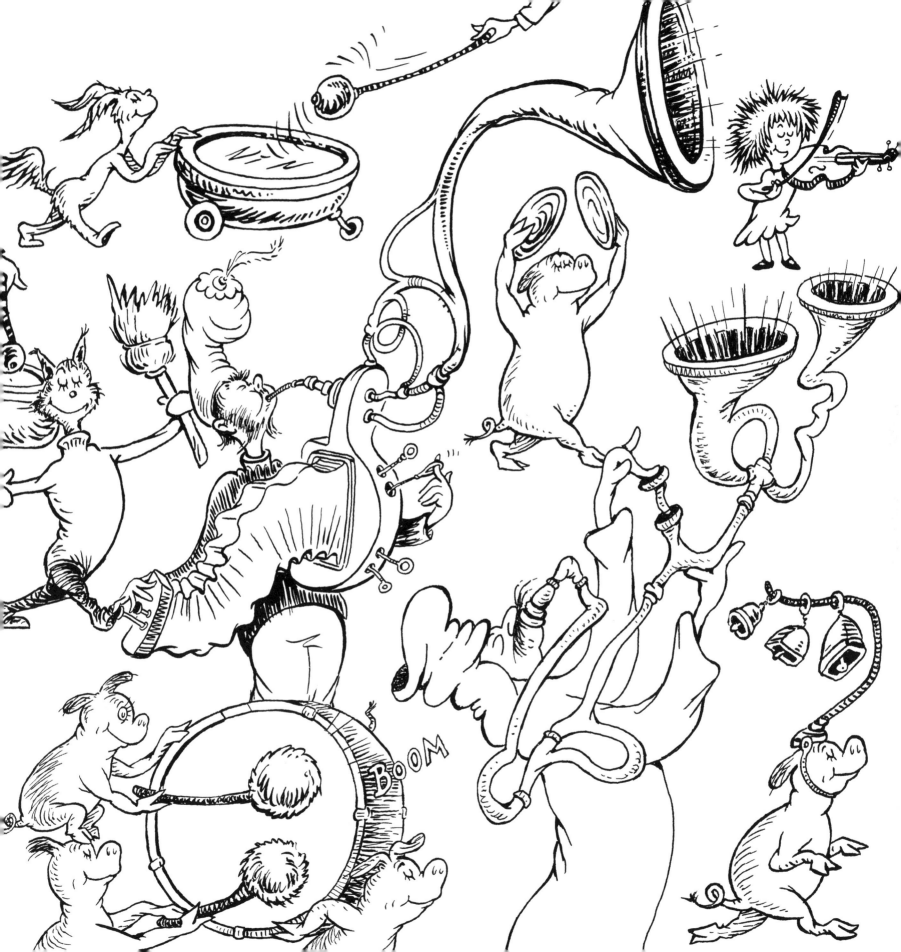

BOOM